MW01140774

The Great Fishing Contest

LANGLEY CHRISTIAN SCHOOL
21789 - 50th Avenue,
Langley, B.C. V3A 3T2
533-2222

The Great Fishing Contest

BY DAVID KHERDIAN

ILLUSTRATED BY NONNY HOGROGIAN

Philomel Books · New York

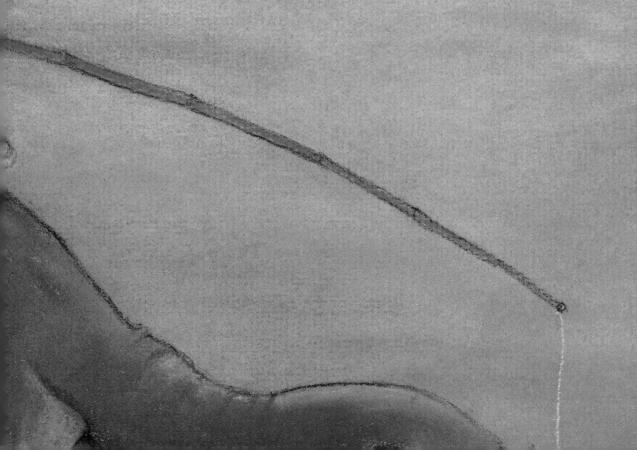

To My Hometown
—D.K.

Text copyright © 1991 by David Kherdian.
Illustrations copyright © 1991 by Nonny H. Kherdian.
Published by Philomel Books, a division of The Putnam & Grosset Book Group,
200 Madison Avenue, New York, NY 10016. All rights reserved.
Published simultaneously in Canada.
Printed in Hong Kong by South China Printing Co. (1988) Ltd.
Book Design by Nonny Hogrogian

Library of Congress Cataloging-in-Publication Data
Kherdian, David.
The great fishing contest / by David Kherdian;
illustrated by Nonny Hogrogian.
p. cm.
Summary: After painstaking preparations with his friend
Sammy, Jason enters the big fishing contest and follows a plan
to discover where the biggest fish in the pond are hiding.
ISBN 0-399-22263-4
[1. Fishing—Fiction. 2. Contests—Fiction.]
I. Hogrogian, Nonny, Ill. II. Title.
PZ7, K527Gr 1991 [Fic]—dc20 90-35397 CIP AC

First Impression

The Great Fishing Contest

One

"School's out" means something different to everybody. To me and Sammy it means three more weeks until The Great Fishing Contest. That's our name for it. I'm not sure it has an official name, unless it's something like "the fishing contest at the zoo pond for children under twelve on July 3rd from 12 noon to 2 P.M."

But that doesn't begin to get into the details, and details are what everything is about.

For one thing, the first prize is a complete spinning outfit. That's the first and most important detail. That's the best part of the contest, but in another way it's the worst. Because if I win the first prize it means that Sammy won't. And if Sammy wins, I don't. Either way, this would be enough to spoil the contest for *both* of us, and that's why we had to put our heads together right at the beginning and figure out what we would do if one of us actually *got* the first prize.

"If that happens," I announced one day as we were walking home from school, "we'll get odd jobs until we've made enough money for the other guy to buy a similar outfit."

"Let's shake on it, Jason," Sammy said.

And that's what we did, but not before spitting on our palms for good luck.

The day after school let out we walked to the zoo in order to check out the pond. This was probably the 132nd time we'd checked out the pond since we first entered the contest, but that didn't make it any less exciting for either of us. We both knew it was a shallow pond used mainly by young kids for sailing boats, by older kids for skating, and by ducks and geese for wading in and swimming.

"It's a pretty usual pond," Sammy said, as we stood on the bank surveying all of it at a glance.

"Except for one thing," I said, "the footbridge that divides this pond from the fenced-in one that's off-limits."

"Doesn't matter," Sammy answered. "You can't fish from the bridge."

"And you can't fish from the banks because they're too steep."

"And you can't go in the water, and if you *fall* in you're disqualified."

We had walked over to the middle of the footbridge and were staring down at the water beneath it.

"It's so deep here you can't see the bottom," Sammy said.

"What does that mean?"

"It means the biggest fish are probably down there."

"Not necessarily," I said. "There's a screen that divides the two ponds." I could tell Sammy didn't know what I was talking about.

We gave that detail some thought as we turned and walked to the opposite railing and looked out over the pond that was off-limits. This was the pond where the ducks and geese and other birds went when they didn't want to be bothered, like when they were having babies. The fence around the pond wasn't meant to keep them in but to keep us out.

"Do you think those older guys we heard about really took those fourteen-inch bluegills out of there last summer?"

"I don't know, Jason. What do you think?"

I looked out over the off-limits pond and gave it some thought. "It's deep enough," I answered. "It's plenty deep enough to hold some big fish."

"I wouldn't be daring enough to sneak in at night, would you? Even if I could scale that fence."

"I'd give almost anything to catch a fourteen-inch bluegill," I said, avoiding a straight answer.

We turned around and went back to the other railing. "A fourteen-inch bluegill would practically have to swim with his fins out of the water on this side," Sammy announced, as we surveyed the main pond again.

"That's right!" I exclaimed, and all at once I visualized the pond in winter, with the skaters carefully maneuvering between the fins of these huge bluegills that had gotten themselves frozen into place.

12

"What are you thinking, Jason?"

"Did it ever occur to you, Sammy, that this pond freezes solid in the winter?"

"Sure—but so what?"

"Well, there are always enough fish for the contest in the summer, so if the pond freezes solid in the winter, where do they come from? Fish aren't planted, you know."

Sammy gave a start, and then jerked his thumb over his shoulder toward the other pond. "Over there!"

"That's right, which means that the screen under the bridge doesn't go all the way to the bottom, so it keeps people from sneaking into that part of the pond but doesn't keep the fish out of *this* part."

"Remember when we came out here during spring vacation and saw the bluegills with their spawning nests along the bank in the main pond?"

"All smoothed out, with the hollow in the center where the eggs must have been."

"Right! So where do you think those mother bluegills came from?"

"In there," Sammy answered, pointing over his shoulder again. "And I guess that's why the baby blue-gills stay *here,* because if they went back in *there* they'd be eaten by those lunkers."

"I guess the ones that survive the fishing contest are big enough to go back to the off-limits pond by winter-time. And it means there are plenty more where they came from."

"It's quite a system, isn't it?"

"Yeah, and mostly invisible."

Two

I don't know if we had made any headway in our planning for the fishing contest, but we both felt like we had made some discoveries. And we definitely had something to think about.

The reason we were so eager to win the spinning rod was because my dad always said that when we got old enough he'd take us fishing on one of the big lakes outside of town. And old enough to us meant having our own spinning rods, with tackle boxes to match. Sammy and I couldn't afford either one, and since Sammy's parents were divorced, with his dad living in another town, I wasn't going to ask my dad for something—even something I was pretty sure he'd never buy for me—if it meant Sammy couldn't have one too.

The idea was to win that spinning rod, because then my dad would see that we were ready for fishing out of a boat for game fish, and not just pan fish, which was all we were able to do now.

Actually, if the river that ran through our town hadn't been polluted, we probably would have been satisfied to fish there. Once upon a time it had black bass and pickerel, and then later you could still catch rock bass, bluegills and bullheads, but now the only things left are carp and suckers, and it's dangerous to eat them. Sammy and I feel the same way: you shouldn't catch what you don't intend to eat.

The only time we go fishing now is when we hike out to this small lake on the outskirts of town. It's so shallow along the banks, and so crowded with trees, that the only way you can catch any fish is to get out in the middle, where it's still pretty shallow. We have this flotation tube that Sammy got one Christmas that we pump up once we get to the lake, and it's just big enough for the two of us. We have to use very short poles or else we get all tangled up. One time we brought long poles. We floated around the lake, hollering at each other, getting tangled, and arguing about whose turn it was to paddle; it made it impossible to get really serious about fishing. About the only thing that kept us on the job was the promise of a fish fry afterward.

We always bring a couple of potatoes along, plus a little griddle, and of course salt and pepper. We bury the potatoes in the coals of the fire and cook the fish on the griddle, but only after we've done our preparatory work. We have this secret place where we do our cooking that we keep camouflaged, and so far no one's discovered it.

Since two potatoes aren't enough for an outdoor lunch, we *have* to catch fish, and so far we always have, although one time we caught only two small crappies, and there was more ceremony than food to our "outdoor repast" that day. *Repast* is one of those words we picked up from reading the outdoor fishing and hunting magazines, which we do a lot of. We've figured out that the less you do of something the more time you have to spend reading about it, and dreaming about it.

But we'd rather read about fishing than collect baseball cards and dream about being Big Leaguers. We both like exploring and discovering things. Collecting is okay but it takes money, and no matter how much you have of something you always want more. That's especially true of baseball cards. Ask anyone who collects them.

Collecting and adventuring are very definitely two different things.

Three

"We have to decide if it's good luck to try and earn enough money for one spinning rod before the fishing contest. That way if one of us wins the first prize we'll both have a rod." We were having a serious conference in my bedroom, which is where we always go when we have a "major decision" to make. It's the only place we can go where we know we won't be overheard, and my mom's been given strict instructions not to interrupt us unless it's something important, like something she's just baked. Cookies, for instance.

We both went silent and set to thinking. Luck was a detail you couldn't forget, but it was one of the hardest to figure out.

"It could be good luck, and then it could be bad," Sammy answered. "We have to decide."

"Can we get some help with our decision?"

"For instance?"

"My sister opens this book called the *I Ching*, and then she throws a couple of coins, which tell her what to do next."

"How does it work?"

"Beats me."

"Let's not try it, then. Any other ideas?"

"Maybe we can try a little reason instead. If we already have enough money for one rod, maybe luck won't be on our side for the contest."

"Like we're being greedy."

"It could be that wanting too much brings bad luck."

"It wouldn't make sense that greed could bring *good* luck."

21

"I think you're right, it doesn't figure."

"There's another thing, if one of us wins first prize, that might mean we're lucky, and then getting the second rod will be easier because we'll have luck on our side."

"That's right, and it will mean that our luck didn't come from greed. It came from something else."

"It might be best not to know what that other thing is, just in case knowing puts a jinx on it."

"I should have thought of that myself," I said. "It's perfect!"

My mom had to knock twice before we heard her and told her it was okay to come in. Instead of jumping up for the cookies and milk that she was bringing in— like we usually do—we told her to put the tray on the bureau. She looked at us kind of funny but didn't say anything until she got to the door. "A couple of deep thinkers," she mumbled as she closed the door behind her.

Four

"Corks are best," Sammy was saying. We were sitting on his front steps watching the sun go down. There were only two days left until the contest. "With a cork you always know what the fish is doing when it bites. And we both know just when to set the hook, which is more than you can say for most of the kids who go to the contest."

"If you use a cork you can't get the line out as far."

"But with all the small fish around, if you don't use a cork you can lose your bait and not even know you had a bite."

"You have to use a tiny cork—like one of those wine-bottle corks cut in half—and be sure not to put any sinkers on the line. That way they can run more easily with the bait."

"The real question is how to catch the biggest fish. All the other prizes are based on the total weight of all the fish caught, but we want the first prize."

"But since catching the biggest fish is mainly luck, shouldn't we catch as many as we can? That way we're working on the law of averages."

"The law of averages is okay but it's kind of sloppy. Not very scientific, if you ask me."

"If you ask me, the trouble with this contest is that it's too much chance and not enough skill."

"But that's just what I was trying to say. I don't think we're on the same wavelength today, Sammy."

We were silent for a while, mainly because the sun was big, and red, and glorious, and would soon be out of sight.

"I always figure there's a secret to everything," I said. "Knowing how to catch a fish is one thing, but I still say the secret is knowing *where* they are. In this case, where the biggest fish is, or is apt to be."

"I think you're getting over your head. The contest is always won by an eight- or nine-inch fish, and the biggest fish is never more than a half-inch larger than the second biggest fish. Seems to me it's pure luck. Being in the right place at the right time with the right bait. Period."

"But what if that isn't the case?"

The sun had disappeared and put an end to our argument.

Five

It was the day before The Great Fishing Contest. All the other kids were out buying firecrackers and sparklers and all the other junk that goes with the Fourth of July. We hadn't exactly outgrown our love of firecrackers, but they weren't included in our pact to save all the money we could for fishing and exploring.

We were going over the rules one last time. We each had a regulation five-foot pole—any poles longer than that would have resulted in endless tangles and mixed lines. Also you couldn't fish so close that you touched the person next to you. Everyone was allowed to bring a bucket, which could include a can or container for bait because everyone fished with worms. As for extra lines and hooks and bobbers, they had to be carried "on the person."

Most of the contestants didn't bother with bringing extra equipment, but that was not the way with Sammy and me. "We have to be prepared for every eventuality," was how Sammy summed it up. We each had an extra cork, in which we imbedded two hooks. We also carried extra line.

The other rule was that you couldn't change places once the starting flag waved.

And we couldn't forget the most important rule of all: Time. The contest lasted from twelve to two, but you could show up for the contest anytime that day you wanted. Sammy and I planned to get there at least one hour ahead. Everyone said it didn't matter where you fished because the pond was the same from one end to

the other, but everyone knew each spot where the winning fish had been taken since the contest began in 1981, and each person, I suppose, had his own idea of which of those spots was the best.

On this score Sammy had something to say that was pretty smart. "Have you noticed there haven't been any repeats? For that reason alone a guy would be better off going to a different spot than one that's already won."

"You're right," I said, "because in either case it's superstition. I don't think luck has anything to do with it."

We decided we would fish on opposite sides of the pond from each other. That way we could see each other and signal our progress. Sammy had always favored the side of the pond with the life-size statue of an elephant, so I told him I'd take the other side.

Six

We set out from home two hours early the day of the contest, which meant we'd have plenty of time to pick out a spot of our choice. As it turned out we weren't the first ones there, but it didn't really matter because everyone was wandering around and no one had fixed their place as yet.

Sammy and I parted. He went over to the elephant and climbed up and stood on its back. "What do you see?" I shouted.

"Nothing," Sammy shouted back.

"Then get down before you break your neck." Sammy sat down on the elephant's back and then slowly slid off.

I had sat down on the high bank overlooking the pond. It was a hot day, no breeze, and when I looked up at the clock on the big animal den I saw that we had a full hour and a half to go.

There were usually ducks sleeping on the bank, their heads tucked under their wings, but they must have known it was the third of July because they were in the middle of the pond, along with the geese, swimming restlessly in circles. It wouldn't be long, I knew, before they'd fly to the other pond.

My eye kept going to the bridge, and it was several minutes before I realized that there was something stirring in me that I hadn't yet nailed down well enough to understand. Suddenly a voice inside me said, "That's where you've got to fish." Although I was confused by my own statement, I got to my feet and started off in the direction of the bridge.

To my surprise—probably because I had been dreaming—there was a strange girl my age very near the spot I was headed for. I'd never seen her before. I edged around her into the last available spot between her and the bridge. The girl looked at me and screwed up her freckled face, which made two brown ovals on her cheeks. "This is my spot!" she commanded.

"That's right," I said. "You haven't moved."

"That doesn't give you a right to stand on top of me."

"I'm not standing on top of you—and I'm not touching you. I guess you know the rules."

"I guess you know the rules, too—I hope," she said.

I sat down and watched her wave her pole in the air. I rejected three or four choice remarks and lay back on the grass. I closed my eyes. "This is it," I said to myself. "The great day is here. I hope I win the spinning rod, and if I can't win it myself I hope Sammy does. I promise not to brag if I win it or become jealous if Sammy wins it." That was a pretty high order, which was why I made myself promise.

Seven

They had waved the flag. The poles were in the water.
There must have been a hundred kids in the contest, all
boys except for the creature standing next to me. I
couldn't decide if she was bad luck or not, so I made a
point of being the last one to put his line in the water. I
figured if she was bad luck this would cancel it out. I
spit on my bait for extra measure.

I no sooner got my line in the water when my next-door neighbor pulled out her first bluegill. She took it off her hook, dropped it in her bucket, and turned and winked at me. I didn't get it. Was she bragging, was she being friendly, was she being cute, or what?

I couldn't help but notice that she was fishing without a cork. She had a single split shot about five inches up from her hook. I noticed that she retrieved her line very slowly, sometimes stopping altogether. She must have gotten the first one that way, because as I watched I noticed she got another hit. She set the hook a little too soon this time and it got away. She knew her stuff, all right, and I guess she had been letting me know with her wink.

I looked up to see Sammy hauling one in across the pond. Small. Then I got my first bite. The cork hardly rippled the water at first, but all at once it started to drift out—then it went under. I set the hook and had him. He was a good six inches. Probably the biggest one to be caught so far, which didn't mean much, but I guess it meant something.

By now the girl next to me had caught four little ones. She had lost all interest in me, and I was willing to lose all interest in her. She was obviously hoping to catch as many as she could and hope the law of averages was on her side. I was hoping for something else, but I didn't have a plan. Not yet.

I kept eyeing the bridge, and every time I did my eye would travel down to the water, and then my imagination would go down deep *into* the water, where I figured a big fish or two or three were lurking about in the shadows. I didn't have any trouble imagining a fourteen-inch bluegill down there. But I wouldn't need to catch one nearly that big to win the contest. Besides, a fourteen-inch fish would have broken my pole.

Last year the winning fish went nine and a quarter inches, a record. All the other winners had been under nine inches. In fact, the first year the winning fish was just under eight inches. Everyone said the fish were getting bigger since the contest began because the more fish we caught, the more food there was for the ones that were left.

This kind of thinking was doing me absolutely no good. I looked over at the clock. The first hour had gone by. Only one hour to go. I had caught seven fish. The first one was still the biggest. The girl beside me had at least twelve by now, and I almost let myself start wondering if she would win the weight contest, which would probably be good for a tackle box loaded with stuff. "Let her. What's it to me?" I said under my breath. "Second prize is definitely not what you had in mind," the voice concluded, just to remind me, in case I'd forgotten my goal.

Eight

Forty-five minutes to go.

Thirty minutes to go.

I removed my bobber, reached into my can, took out a worm, and put it in my shirt pocket.

It's now or never. Even if no one else knows where the big fish are in this pond, I do. They're right there, in the hole under the bridge. So what was holding me back: fear, embarrassment, stupidity? Yes, and one more thing besides: the rules. If you stepped into the water, even by accident, you were disqualified, and I knew it wouldn't be possible to stand on the bank next to the bridge without slipping into the water. By now I was inching my way over—that is, inching along with my feet. But even with sneakers on, my feet began to slide on the grass. Without planning to I got down on my hands and knees and started crawling, but by the time I got nearly to the edge of the bridge I started sliding again. So I did the only thing I could: I crawled on my stomach until my hands had nearly reached the water's edge. Somehow I managed to fling the line up over my head, but when I brought it down, my pole slapped the water and made a noise that could be heard from one end of the pond to the other.

The freckle-faced girl started screaming at once. "He's cheating! He's cheating!"

"There's nothing in the rule books about standing or sitting," I screamed back.

"How about crawling?" she shouted back.

"Crawling neither," I hollered.

I had caught the time out of the corner of my eye: ten minutes before two. All eyes were on me but no one else had said a word.

Just then I felt a tug, and when I looked at my pole I could see the tip being pulled toward the bridge—and I could feel a fish on the line. I gave a jerk as best I could in the position I was in, but what happened next almost stopped my breath. *I couldn't pull my pole out of the water.* The weight at the other end was too great. At first I thought I had a shark or a whale on the line—or maybe a fourteen-inch bluegill—but then I knew what it was: the fish had pulled my line under the wire fence, and instead of setting the hook, as I had thought, I had pulled it out of his mouth and my hook had caught in the mesh wiring.

I jerked and jerked, but nothing happened. By now I was lying on my side, and I thought to turn my head and look at the clock. It was five minutes before two. I pulled my pole, hand over hand until I had the line in my grasp, and I began pulling it as hard as I could. If I lost too much of my line I wouldn't have time to restring another, and so I prayed that the hook would break off. And that's what happened. Lying on my back, I reached inside my pocket, took out my extra cork, pulled off one of the hooks, reached into my shirt pocket and got my worm.

This was it, two minutes to go. If I missed the next one—if there was a next one—I would be out of time. But they were there, and they hadn't been fished for before. *And so here I go,* I said under my breath, as I flipped my pole over my head while rolling over on my stomach.

Seconds went by and nothing happened—and once again I felt the tug and could see my pole being jerked at the tip as the fish made its way under the bridge with my bait in its mouth. *Last chance, don't panic,* I told myself, as I held out till the last possible moment before setting the hook. This time I had the fish, not the fence, and I knew it. He was on—and he was BIG!

But now what? How was I to get him in? First on my back, and then on my stomach, I tried to pull him in over my head, but I just couldn't get the leverage I needed. I had to crawl for it, back the way I came. But would there be time? I looked up at the clock. Less than a minute to go. Old freckle-face saw me eyeing the clock. "You'll never make it, you'll never make it!"

It looked like my time was up but I couldn't be sure. I went faster, faster—and at last I reached level ground. Pulling with all my might, I watched as my fish broke water—just as the white flag began to wave from across the pond. And all at once a cheer went up. I was sure I had won! I had won!

"That's a record," I heard the girl saying. "I knew you could do it."

When I looked up from my beached fish—which had to be at least ten inches—I heard Sammy hollering in the distance. I looked up to see him waving his arms and running as fast as he could in my direction.